Follow

the Way of

Love

MARY JO DANNELS

ISBN 978-1-64003-422-8 (Paperback)
ISBN 978-1-64003-423-5 (Digital)

Covenant Books, Inc.
11661 Hwy 707
Murrells Inlet, SC 29576
www.covenantbooks.com

Dedication

This book is dedicated to my father, Gerald Henry Jenkins. He taught me the *way of love*, the *most excellent way*. He taught me by his words, yes, but mostly by his actions. I watched him read the word of God, and I watched him put them into practice in his everyday life, every day of the fifty-one years of his life.

I would also like to thank my husband, Fred Dannels, and son Benjamin Dannels for their support throughout this process. And, of course, my son Jacob Dannels, whose life was an inspiration to all who knew him, in using your words and following your dreams.

Preface

When my son was in preschool, his classmates kept touching his flattop haircut. It was really very annoying to my son, so I wrote a note to his teacher. She gave my son the best advice: "Use your words."

So we practiced using his words. How empowering to a four-year old to know that what he speaks out of his mouth can change his circumstances. This book takes this a step further and combines the power of what you speak with the Word of God. My book is based on 1 Corinthians 13, which is often called the "love chapter," and is read at the majority of weddings I've attended. My thought process is that it is wonderful to start a marriage based on this. But why not start our children out in life based on the words from the love chapter? It really is, as Saint Paul says, "the most excellent way"!

Love is patient. It never gives up.

"I am patient. I never give up!" I can practice being patient when I wait in line. Sometimes it's hard to be patient, but when it's finally my turn, it's so much fun!

Jesus compared patience to a farmer waiting for his plants to grow. Plants take a long time to grow. But they *do* grow! And sometimes waiting for something very special can be fun too. Just thinking about how wonderful it will be is a great way to be patient!

"I am patient. I never give up."

Love is kind. Love cares more for others than for self.

"I am kind. I care more for others than for myself."

It's easy to always think about me, but being kind to others is also very easy and makes you feel good inside. I can be kind by smiling at people. I can be kind by helping someone open a door. I can be kind by saying "thank you" and telling someone how wonderful they are. Lots of times when you smile at someone, they smile back! Or if someone has their hands full and you open the door, they are so happy. If someone is having a bad day and I am kind to them, it makes everyone's day better.

"I am kind. I care more for others than myself."

Love does not boast.
Love is down-to-earth.

"I am down-to-earth. You are very special!"

It is nice when people say nice things about us, and when they do, we should always say "thank you." And while it is nice to be told this, we must be very careful not to think of ourselves as better than others. Every person is very special and unique. God made each of us in an extraordinary way. It's so good to look at others for their special qualities and say nice things about them. "I am down-to-earth. You are special."

Love is not proud.
Love is humble.

"I am humble."

Humble is a good word to learn and a great way to be. Sort of like when someone keeps telling you how great you are to do what you do, but you know it really is very easy, and what you do is good because God is helping you. It is a knowing that it isn't you who is actually so great, but it is our God who is so *great*. To thank people for their nice comments and then thank God who helps us every day is a good way to be humble. "I am humble."

Love is not rude.
Love is gentle.

"I am gentle."

When I think about being gentle and not rude, I think about how I am with a little kitten or around a newborn baby. Quiet, soft hands and inside voice. Sometimes gentle is a whisper, and sometimes it's a tiptoe. It is not yelling loud and stomping around.

"I am gentle."

Love is not self-seeking.
Love is selfless.

"I am selfless."

Our words are getting complicated. It is a "selfie" world we are living in. Being selfless is like taking pictures of other people and not being in the picture yourself. To be selfless is to focus on others and think about them and what would make them happy.

"I am selfless."

Love is not easily angered.
Love is calm.

"I am calm."

I've heard it said that *calm* is a superpower! To be calm, sometimes it helps to listen to yourself breathe ten times. It's so easy to be angry sometimes, but if you breathe in deeply and ask God to help you, then you can be calm. I like the words "practice calm, delight!"

"I am calm."

Love keeps no record of wrongs. Love remembers all of the good things.

"I remember all of the good things."

Bad things happen sometimes. Good things also happen. Sometimes we are treated wrong, but we are also treated right. When you feel sad, try to make a list of all of the good things that have happened. It will always make you feel better.

"I remember all of the good things."

Love does not delight in evil
but rejoices with the truth!

"I rejoice with the truth!"

The truth is what happened. It will never change. The truth is. Be happy with the truth. Do not lie; it never helps anyone to lie.

"I rejoice with the truth. The truth makes me happy."

Love always believes the best of every person.

"I always believe the best of every person."

I believe everyone is trying their very best. Sometimes we might think they can do better, but we don't always know what else is happening to that person. God knows, and we can pray for God to help them. They are the very best version of themselves that they can be.

"I always believe the best of every person."

Love always trusts.

"I trust God always."

I rely on God to help me in all ways with everything. He is my rock; He does not move. Always, all ways!

"I trust God in all my ways!"

Love always perseveres.

"I always persevere. I stick with it and I finish what I start."

It's easy and fun to start something new. Then it's easy and fun to start something else that is new. If you want to persevere, you *must* finish what you start! It's not always as fun and easy, but it is a very good feeling when you finish and see what you have completed.

"I always persevere. I stick with it, and I finish what I start."

Love always hopes.

"I always hope."

When I hope, I expect very good things to happen. I hope with joy. I like the words *joyfully expectant*. That's how I hope—with a big smile on my face!

"I always hope."

Love never fails.
Love thrives and succeeds!

"I thrive and succeed. I win!"

I like to say I do my very best always. When I do my very best, then I succeed. I thrive, and I grow.

"I thrive and succeed. I win!"

Follow the way of love! It is the most excellent way!

About the Author

Mary Jo Dannels is a mother of two and lives in Pennsylvania with her husband, Fred. She enjoys journaling, knitting, and gardening. This is her first book, and she is excited to share her beautiful message of love.

CPSIA information can be obtained
at www.ICGtesting.com
Printed in the USA
BVHW02s1121290418
514754BV00026B/690/P

9 781640 034228